culous

THE SWEET AND LOVELY ROYALS OF

CLASSROOM 13

DISCARD

By **Honest Lee** & **Matthew J. Gilbert**
Art by **Joelle Dreidemy**

Ⓛ Ⓑ

LITTLE, BROWN AND COMPANY
New York • Boston

Little, Brown and Company
Hachette Book Group
1290 Avenue of the Americas, New York, NY 10104
Visit us at LBYR.com

First Edition: November 2018

Little, Brown and Company is a division of Hachette Book Group, Inc. The Little, Brown name and logo are trademarks of Hachette Book Group, Inc.

The publisher is not responsible for websites (or their content) that are not owned by the publisher.

Library of Congress Cataloging-in-Publication Data
Names: Lee, Honest, author. | Gilbert, Matthew J., author. | Dreidemy, Joelle, illustrator.
Title: The rude and ridiculous royals of Classroom 13 / by Honest Lee & Matthew J. Gilbert ; art by Joelle Dreidemy.
Description: First edition. | New York : Little, Brown and Company, 2018. | Series: Classroom 13 ; book 6 | Summary: The students of Classroom 13 become kings and queens and create outrageous laws.
Identifiers: LCCN 2017044922| ISBN 9780316437882 (hardcover) | ISBN 9780316437868 (trade pbk.) | ISBN 9780316437875 (ebook) | ISBN 9780316437899 (library ebook edition)
Subjects: | CYAC: Kings, queens, rulers, etc.—Fiction. | School field trips—Fiction. | Schools—Fiction. | Humorous stories.
Classification: LCC PZ7.1.L415 Ru 2018 | DDC [Fic]—dc23
LC record available at https://lccn.loc.gov/2017044922

ISBNs: 978-0-316-43788-2 (hardcover), 978-0-316-43786-8 (paperback), 978-0-316-43787-5 (ebook)

Printed in the United States of America

LSC-H

10 9 8 7 6 5 4 3 2 1

 CONTENTS

You might need this later....
You're welcome.

-Honest Lee

YUNA'S ATBASH CIPHER:

A	B	C	D	E	F	G	H	I	J	K	L	M
Z	Y	X	W	V	U	T	S	R	Q	P	O	N

CHAPTER 1
The Fun Field Trip

When very unlucky schoolteacher Ms. Linda LaCrosse woke up Monday morning, she hoped it would be another uneventful day. That is, until she remembered what today was...."It's *field trip day!*"

Ms. Linda hopped out of bed and danced around her room, singing. She hit such a high note with her voice that the bedroom window shattered. Four birds flew in and chased Ms. Linda around the room.

Eventually, she managed to lock the birds in her bedroom. Then she ate breakfast in the shower and showered in the kitchen. Afterward, she found it odd that she'd made such a mess.

I did say Ms. Linda was rather unlucky. Yet she remained a happy and hopeful teacher. As she drove to school, she said, "Today, I hope nothing *weird* happens with my students when we go to the museum."

Silly Ms. Linda. She should have known that by saying such a thing out loud, she just jinxed herself.

When Ms. Linda got to school, the field trip day was already off to a bad start. First, Sophia tried to sneak the class hamster, Earl, onto the bus. Ms. Linda insisted *no* animals could go on the field trip.

While the teacher was distracted, Mason snuck his cow, Touchdown, onto the bus. He put Touchdown in a wig and a sweater. Ms. Linda saw her and said, "Oh, you must be Mandy, my new teacher's assistant. It's a pleasure to have you."

Touchdown said, "*Moo!*"

"Nice to *moo* you, too," Ms. Linda replied.

They were going to be late if they didn't leave soon. But they were waiting on one last student: Santiago. As he finally *rolled* up to the bus, he was all puffy with bright green spots. He was also inside a big plastic bubble.

"Why are you inside a balloon?" Ms. Linda asked.

"I'm sick," Santiago sniffled, "but I refuse to miss a field trip just because I caught a nasty stomach-throat-skin virus. Don't worry, my quarantine bubble will protect everyone while I'm contagious."

"I think maybe you should go home," Ms. Linda said.

Santiago refused. "No way. Field trips are the best! I won't miss it."

Ms. Linda didn't want to deny any of her students a chance to learn. So she let him board the bus.

"Is everyone here?" Ms. Linda asked.

Everyone shouted, "Yes!" Which was true. All twenty-seven students were present—including the newest student in Classroom 13. Actually, the new student *is* Classroom 13. You see, the 13th Classroom was tired of missing out on the wild and zany adventures, and so *it* (the classroom) *became* a student. If you're wondering how, don't ask me. I don't understand physics. If you're wondering if 13 is a *he* or a *she*—it is neither. It's an *it*.

Don't look at *me* like that! I just wrote the book. If Classroom 13 wants to be a *he*, or a *she*, or an *it*, it's not up to me, it's up to *it*!

Anyways...

The bus ride was only a few hours long, and

the students were surprisingly quiet. Ms. Linda appreciated how well behaved they were—until she realized why.

Of the twenty-seven present students, *all of them* were on their phones. One was taking photos, two were reading celebrity news, three were watching movies, and four were playing video games. The remaining seventeen students were texting each other. (They thought it was far more fun to text than to talk, even when seated next to each other.)

"Could everyone please put their phones away?" Ms. Linda asked. All the students groaned. "A field trip is an excellent way to gain firsthand knowledge."

"Is 'gain firsthand knowledge' the same thing as 'learning'?" Preeya asked.

"Why, yes it is," Ms. Linda answered.

All the students groaned again—except Olivia. She liked learning.

"Where are we going?" Isabella asked.

"To a museum!" Ms. Linda said. "We're going to learn about castles and catapults and maidens and knights and kings and queens."

"I'm bored already," Zoey said. "Can we go do something fun instead?"

"This *will* be fun," Ms. Linda said. "We'll get to see old paintings and sculptures and chandeliers and rugs—"

"*Snores*-ville!" Liam said.

"We'll also get to see how laws were made in the past," Ms. Linda added. "You see, in the old days, it was up to the kings and queens to make laws with the help of their courts. Some of those laws laid the groundwork for laws that we use today."

"Laws are dumb," William said.

"Yeah," most of the kids agreed.

"If *we* were the kings and queens, we'd make things so much better!" said Isabella.

"*Yeah!*" all the kids shouted.

Ms. Linda thought this might be what teachers call a "teachable moment"—which means an event that presents a chance for learning. So she said, "Then please tell me—if you could be a king or a queen for the day—what laws would you make?"

"*If?*" 13 laughed. "There's no need to say *if*— not when *I* can make it really happen."

The new student with a cube for a head stood up and snapped its fingers. There was a big burst of magical light...

CHAPTER 2
The Freaky Field Trip

••• and as the school bus pulled up in front of the castle, a huge crowd was waiting. The people were holding signs that said WELCOME, KINGS AND QUEENS OF CLASSROOM 13!

A huge crowd of people stood on either side of a red carpet. A band played music while vendors sold flags. There was even a group of security guards waiting to escort the students inside.

"What is going on?!" Ms. Linda asked.

13 smiled. (Well, kinda—13 doesn't have a mouth.) "Oh, I made your *hypothetical* question into a *real* reality."

"But how?"

"I have magic powers," 13 said.

"Well, can you *undo* it?" Ms. Linda said. "The field trip is a way of learning."

"So is being an *actual* queen or king," 13 said.

"We want to be kings!" the boys shouted.

"We want to be queens!" the girls shouted.

"Girls in charge of a country? Ridiculous." Jacob laughed. "I'm pretty sure that's not even legal!"

Zoey, Yuna, Ximena, Sophia, Preeya, Olivia, Mya & Madison, Lily, Isabella, Fatima, Emma, Chloe, and Ava all leapt up and punched Jacob in the arm.

Ms. Linda turned bright red. "Oh my! Jacob, how did you not know? Women are *of course* equal to men. I guess you students *do* need to learn about kings and queens. I suppose we can try this, 13—but only until I say when."

"Fantastic," 13 said. "Let's go get our crowns!"

The students from Classroom 13 stepped off the bus. Their security team escorted them into the castle. As the students walked, they waved to their adoring public. People cheered and clapped and screamed. "We love you, kings and queens of Classroom 13!"

Some of the students enjoyed the attention. Others did not. But all of them were excited to rule a country. And all of them were excited to start making (and breaking) the laws.

As they entered the royal throne room, each student was given a golden crown. The kids started jumping and screaming with joy. Ms. Linda said, "Let's all calm down a little. You may be royalty now, but you're still my students. Perhaps we should make laws in alphabetical order. Ava, that means you're first."

"Excellent!" Ava said. "I know just the law I want to make...."

Ms. Linda took several deep breaths as her first student took the throne. Ava was now queen of the country, and she could make any law she wanted to. Ms. Linda feared for the country—and rightly so.

CHAPTER 3
Ava

That's right. As soon as Ava took the throne, she said the three words that every student on the planet had always wanted to hear:

"NO MORE HOMEWORK!"

And just like that, it was made into a law. Word went out to the entire nation. All teachers were to immediately cease giving homework to their students.

Previously, Ava had nothing against school. In fact, she liked school a lot. But she did *not* like having to do schoolwork outside of school. Her parents already had her taking tennis lessons, kicking karate butt, and splashing at swim class. The last thing she wanted to do at the end of a long day was more work. So she outlawed homework.

As word spread, you could hear students everywhere celebrating. College kids cried with contentment at campus parties. High schoolers howled happily. Middle schoolers mooned the moon. Elementary classes expressed their excitement with elongated echoes of elation. And preschoolers—well, preschoolers never had homework, so they just took naps.

Ava was known as a national hero. That first night, she texted her friends on her phone. The second night, she enjoyed a movie marathon with her family. On the third night, she painted a portrait. On the fourth, she read a book. But on the fifth, she had a strange feeling.

"What's wrong?" Teo asked.

"I feel weird," Ava said. "There's all this free time I have, but I don't know what to do with it."

"Oh," Teo said, "you're just *bored*."

"Bored?!" Ava was confused. She'd never been bored before. But she quickly decided being *bored* was better than being *buried* under homework.

When Ava woke up the next morning, she went out on her royal balcony. The crowds booed and hissed at her. They even threw rotten tomatoes. She ran inside and turned on the news. A reporter said, "Ava is one of the worst queens ever. Her new no-homework law has grades dropping. Our country is fast becoming the slowest-learning country in the world. People are dumber than ever! Thanks a lot, Ava."

As her last act as queen, Ava (reluctantly, and with a heavy heart) undid the law. Students everywhere were devastated.

CHAPTER 4
Benji

Benji's crown was decorated with jewels that looked like soccer balls. Some of the kids had to get used to wearing the heavy crowns. But not Benji. As one of the most athletic kids in school, he was familiar with heavy headgear: football helmets, batting helmets, hockey masks, lacrosse headgear, you name it.

You see, Benji loved sports—even if his family didn't.

If Benji wasn't playing sports, he was watching them on TV...at least when he could. After all, some sports channels cost extra money, and they aren't cheap. And his parents refused to pay for them.

"*Two hundred dollars* to watch guys in tights chase a ball?!" his father shrieked. "I'm not paying for that!"

"Maybe the hockey channel, then?!" Benji begged. "It's only seventy-nine dollars." He quietly added: "*For the first two months, plus additional fees, then full-season price activates for the low cost of three hundred dollars. Rules and restrictions apply.*"

Mr. Bearenstein heard that. "Why do you want to waste money watching ice skaters chase a hamburger patty around?"

"It's not a hamburger patty, Dad. It's called a 'puck,'" Benji explained.

"The answer is no. With so many channels,

you wouldn't know what to watch. It would be like throwing cash down the toilet! When you get a job, you can order any ridiculous sports package you want."

Well, now Benji did have a job...as king! He wasted no time making his first royal demand: ***"I want ALL the sports channels!"*** (Sure, it wasn't really a law, but it's what the king wanted.)

That afternoon, a humongous TV satellite was placed in Benji's royal room. He turned on the TV, grabbed his favorite sports drink, and sat back, ready to enjoy all the fancy sports channels his heart desired.

There was just one little problem...well, more like *eight thousand* little problems. There are over *eight thousand* sports being played across the globe every day. (For real, look it up!) And somehow, each had its very own TV channel.

There were the sports everyone knows, like soccer, tennis, and golf. But as the channels got

higher, the sports got weirder: competitive tree climbing, gymnastic tuba playing, full-contact ribbon dancing, something called *curling*.

"I don't know what curling is, but I'm glad I have the Deluxe Curling Channel!" Benji said. "What else is on?"

Benji couldn't decide what to watch. For every one sport he could watch, he was missing at least 7,999 other ones. That didn't seem like such a good deal after all. Certainly not one fit for a king.

So he changed channels constantly. He did this for hours. He flipped through so many new sports channels, his thumb started to hurt. So he hired an assistant just to change the channel for him. This person's official job title was "Royal Channel Changer."

But even with help, he couldn't watch everything. "Ugh!" Benji groaned. "I don't know what to waaaaaatch!"

"Told ya," his dad said.

Benji didn't watch the news. But if he had, he would have seen the media joking that King Benji was the star athlete of a new sport: extreme channel surfing.

CHAPTER 5

Chloe

Do you know what a "vegan" is?

No, it is *not* an alien from the planet Vega. Guess again.

No, it is *not* me trying to type "Megan" and getting my *m*'s and *v*'s mixed up. (But your guesses could certainly use ivpromevent.)

Stop guessing—I'll just tell you!

A vegan is a person who does not eat or use animal products. It's true. A good vegan will never know the thrill of devouring a pepperoni pizza. They will never dine in a steakhouse. And they often cover their eyes when a commercial for fried chicken comes on.

Vegans only eat "things that come from the earth." You know, like corn, carrots, lettuce, potatoes, radishes—all stuff that grows out of dirt.

Anyways, Chloe is a vegan—which should come as no surprise. After all, Chloe is Classroom 13's most eco-friendly student. She spends every waking moment outside of school doing her part to protect the planet and the creatures that live on it. And she doesn't like that people eat animals three times a day. It upsets her. So her first order as queen was to—

"Ahem, I'm a *king*," she said.

"But you're a girl," Preeya said. "Girls *can't* be kings."

"Girls can be anything they want! And who said I was a girl anyway? From here forth, call me *King* Chloe!"

No one could argue with the king, so they called her King Chloe.

Now, as I was saying, Chloe's first order as *king* was to make a new law that some might find hard to swallow. She announced to the nation, ***"From now on, all of you shall live as vegans! No more meat eating!"***

Well! I don't have to tell you that more than half the population did not like this new law—not one bit. Millions of people like to eat meat. Immediately, they began protests outside the castle. All the folks who loved egg-and-bacon breakfasts, lunch meat at lunchtime, and ~~dead animal~~ meat loaf for dinner? They were furious they couldn't eat those things anymore. And those people included Chloe's parents.

"Chloe Kennedy Canter!" her mom growled. "We've always supported you, your protesting, and your veganism—even when we didn't agree with it. I went out of my way to make veggie options just for you on Family Pizza Night. But now you've taken away our choice of pepperoni! We are furious!"

"You always said meat-eaters and non-meat-eaters could live together in harmony, but what about the animals?" King Chloe asked. "You may disagree with me now, but soon you'll love being vegan. Have you even tried tofu?"

Her dad tried it and spit it out. "It doesn't taste like anything!" And he wasn't the only one. Her classmates could barely understand how being a vegan worked.

"Can I eat nachos?" Mark asked.

"No! Nachos have cheese on them! Cheese comes from milk, which comes from cows!" King Chloe said.

"What about cake? Surely you'll say 'Let them eat cake,' right?" Fatima asked.

"No! Cake has eggs in it, and eggs come from chickens!" King Chloe said.

"How about double bacon burgers?" Liam asked.

"NO, NO, NO! Bacon comes from pigs, and beef comes from cows!" King Chloe yelled.

Liam started to cry. "No, it's wrong! A life without nachos and cakes and burgers and bacon is *just plain wrong*."

"I don't mind trying something new," Ms. Linda said, "but *what* are we allowed to eat as vegans?"

King Chloe's royal chef made a sampling of vegan foods. Beef-less burgers. Chicken-less chicken salad. Fake bacon. As they tried it, most of the kids spit it out. "It tastes like cardboard!"

"Perfect! Cardboard comes from paper, which comes from trees!" Chloe noted.

Chloe's classmates hated this new law. Several of them (I won't say who) came up with an idea to get rid of the vegan law. After Chloe went to sleep, they called her parents and reminded them of something parents love to do....

The following day, Chloe's parents marched to the castle and called King Chloe outside. "You're grounded, young lady!"

"I'm not a lady—I'm a king!" Chloe declared.

"Well, you're still grounded. Come on. We're going home. You might be a king, but we're still your parents!"

Chloe was grounded for a whole month. That may sound like a harsh punishment, but at least she got to choose her meals while she served her time: veggie pizza, avocado toast, and...whatever that brown thing is.

"It's a piece of chocolate cake," Chloe said.

"It doesn't taste like chocolate cake," Mason said.

"Well, it's vegan cake. It doesn't have milk or eggs or butter, but it's still really delicious."

"If you say so."

CHAPTER 6
Dev

When it was his turn to be king, Dev didn't notice. In fact, he didn't notice anything because he hadn't looked up from his phone for days. He was so focused on playing (and beating) the new *Teddy Bear Bashers* mobile game, he didn't bother to pay attention to the real world.

"Dev?" Ms. Linda said. "Can you put your game away, please?"

He tapped furiously on his phone screen. "Can't talk! Playing! About to beat level forty-nine!"

"But now's your chance to *lead* the *nation* as king!"

With all his concentration on the video game, Dev thought she said: "But now's your chance to *eat* the *crustacean and onion rings.*"

Dev didn't look up from his game. "No, thanks. I don't really like crab or onion rings."

Ms. Linda wondered, *What do onion rings have to do with anything?*

"He's seeing onion rings that aren't there," Ms. Linda concluded. "Video games have *fried* that boy's mind."

CHAPTER 7
Emma

Every king and queen has a defining moment. King Arthur pulled a sword out of a stone. Queen Isabella I of Spain sent Christopher Columbus on his map-changing voyage. Henry VIII beheaded two of his wives. And Queen Elizabeth I brought about a Golden Age. Today Queen Emma of Classroom 13 was about to put a pet in every single home around the country.

Queen Emma announced from the royal podium: "Our country's newest law: *Each and every household must own a pet.*"

The reporters below all started shouting their questions: "But what if people have allergies?" "What do we name our pets?" "Who's gonna pick up all the pet poop?!"

Emma answered the questions in order. "Allergy medicine will be provided. You can name your pet anything you want. But each of you will be responsible for your pet. Yes, that means picking up lots of poop, but it also means feeding it, petting it, loving it, and posting cute pics of it online for all of us to look at and go, '*Awwwwwwwwwww! Wook at dat widdle furry face.*'"

"Now every kid can have a pet," Emma said. "No matter what their parents say." Emma couldn't wait to meet her *two* new pets. Yes, I said *two* pets.

Emma's royal rule had all kinds of legal stuff that stated, "Each household must have at least one pet *per household*." And since Emma's parents were divorced and lived in two different houses, that meant she had *two* different houses, and thus *two* different pets.

I don't have to tell you that she felt like a total genius for figuring this out. Emma had always wanted a cat, and now she was going to get *two* of them. *TWO!* (And *with* allergy medicine, which was good because she was super allergic.)

Emma was so happy, she did cartwheels.

Her parents did *not* do cartwheels. They were *not* happy.

But there was nothing they could do. Their daughter was queen, and now the happy owner of two fluffy kittens: a gray one she named Cleo and a tuxedo-colored one she named Pepe A. Snuggleman, Purr-veyor of Snuggles.

She couldn't wait to show them to her friends. They were all going to be jealous! But when she walked through the castle door, it turns out they weren't jealous at all.

Liam had a llama, Mason had a monkey, and Ethan had an elephant! Chloe had a crocodile, Fatima had a flamingo, and Zoey had a zebra! Everyone in Classroom 13 picked super-rare, exotic animals that their parents would *never* have allowed them to adopt before Emma's new law.

"Thanks, Emma!" everyone shouted. Everyone loved her new law. Everyone except Emma.

Emma hated to admit it, but *she* was the one who was jealous. After seeing everyone else's cool pets, she found herself wishing she'd used her imagination a bit more. She could have had a sea turtle, or a red panda, or a fennec fox.

Or, at least, *bigger* cats.

Ms. Linda had a new pet tiger! *A tiger!!*

Emma sighed, saying, "My royal plans have ended in total *cat*-astrophe."

CHAPTER 8
Ethan

Ethan usually couldn't make up his mind about anything. But that all changed when he became king.

"For the first time in my life, I know exactly what I want," he announced to the public. "I want to *veto* Chloe's vegan law."

"Veto," my dear reader, means to reject or undo another law.

The nation cheered.

"In its place, *I'm making it mandatory for people to eat ice cream for breakfast, lunch, and dinner!*" Ethan proclaimed. "I'm going to lead by example, of course, and start eating ice cream right now."

Ethan spent the next several days stuffing his face with scoop after scoop of ice cream. We're talking vanilla, chocolate, strawberry, rocky road, mint chocolate chip, cookie dough chunk, tutti-frutti, banana, bacon, peanut butter, dark cherry, and stracciatella (which is just a fancy way of saying chocolate chip), to name just a few.

That weekend, when he went to lie down, he burped and warm liquid cream came up in his throat. "*I think I'm going to be sick,*" he whispered.

And he was. The king spent the night on the throne—and I don't mean the royal throne. No, I mean the *other* throne, the *porcelain* one....

(The toilet.)

Ethan had never felt so awful. When he stopped barfing (and you know...barfing out of his bottom), he appeared on the royal balcony to announce he was undoing his ice cream law.

"It turns out there *is* such a thing as *too much of a good thing*. So I've decided people should just decide for themselves what they want to eat," Ethan said. "I'm banning food laws forever. You want to be vegan, be vegan. You want to eat meat, eat meat. You want to eat ice cream every day? Well, I wouldn't recommend it. But first make sure you're not lactose intolerant."

CHAPTER 9
Fatima

"**W**hat if I don't want to be queen?" Fatima asked.

Ms. Linda was confused. *Didn't every kid want to be in charge?* Ms. Linda didn't know how to answer, so she looked to ~~Touchdown~~ Mandy, the new teacher's assistant, who looked at the castle's garden grass—then started eating it.

(Ms. Linda still hadn't realized her teacher's assistant was a cow. You see, teachers are too busy looking after children to notice such things.)

"Mandy must think Chloe's vegan law is still in effect," Ms. Linda said to herself.

13 walked up to Fatima. "I know I haven't been human very long, but why wouldn't you want to tell everyone what to do?"

"Too much responsibility," Fatima answered. "I'd rather read comic books. Comics are like books, but with fewer words and more pictures. Plus, they're all action and adventure and awesomeness all the time. Comics transport me to another world, where anything's possible. I *wish* every kid could have access to comic books—"

"What did I say about *wishing* for things?!" Ms. Linda cried. (She still had bad dreams about ~~djinns~~ genies in magic lamps.)

Suddenly, Fatima had an idea.

"I will be a queen. ***And my first law will be to open free comic book libraries around the nation for everyone to read any comic book they choose!***"

Comic book libraries began to appear in every city. At first, parents didn't want their kids to go. They'd say, "Comics aren't literature!"

But librarians explained that "all books are books!"

Soon, more people than ever were reading, including the other students from Classroom 13.

"I like the ones where the bad guy is the hero," Liam said, reading *Super-Mean Vampire Villains*.

"For me, it's all about outer space adventures," Lily said, reading *Astro-Bats from Planet Mars*.

"*Mooooo!*" said Ms. Linda's teaching assistant. ~~Touchdown~~ Mandy didn't read, but she was eating the latest issue of *The Pet-tastic Adventures of Fur Force!*

The nation cheered for Fatima. Even people who didn't like reading enjoyed reading comic books. Everyone—from mayors to barbers to garbage collectors to parents—found a comic they loved.

Except for 13. It kept trying to read them, but its head would light up red. "How do I know which bubble to read first?!"

"Top to bottom, and left to right," Fatima said. "Unless it's Arabic, Hebrew, or manga. Then you read right to left."

"Yeah, that's not confusing at all," 13 grumbled. "Whatever happened to good old books *without* pictures? I like those."

CHAPTER 10
Hugo

Comme Hugo était français, il trouvait ridicule qu'on appelle les frites "French fries" parce que les frites n'ont pas été inventées en France. Les "French fries" viennent en fait de Belgique, où, d'après les historiens, les pommes de terre étaient frites dès le XVIIe siècle.

Après être devenu roi, Hugo créa une loi qui interdisait que les pommes de terre frites portent le

nom de "French fries." Dorénavant, on devait appeler les frites tout simplement "fries" ou encore "Belgian fries," mais absolument jamais "French fries."

Tout le monde ignora cette loi.

CHAPTER 11
Isabella

As soon as she took her crown, Isabella commanded: *"Cars are now illegal—ride horses instead!"*

The queen claimed to have put this law into effect because "cars pollute the air with their gas fumes," and "oil is a shrinking resource," and "the world should be concerned for the environment." But I think it was really just because Isabella is obsessed with horses.

Within days, every car and truck and SUV was taken off the road. The nation's highways and roads filled up with horses of every color and shape. Grown-ups rode stallions to their jobs, while kids rode ponies to school. Horses stopped at red lights and trotted forward at green lights. Best of all, no car accidents!

Seeing all the horses galloping together was a beautiful sight, like a scene out of a fairy tale. "This is the best day of my life," Queen Isabella said. "Even better than that time I got a unicorn!" But like most fairy tales, there was something wicked coming...in the air.

You see, true to the queen's word, no cars on the roads meant no more fumes. Well, no more *exhaust* fumes.

There were, however, *poop* fumes. And they stunk real bad.

Highways and byways and toll roads were covered in horse poop. Driveways and parking lots? More horse poop. Intersections and cross-walks? Still more horse poop.

Why, you ask? Simple. Horses go to the bath-room *wherever* and *whenever* they feel like it.

Horses aren't like you or me; they don't go to the toilet and flush. They don't worry about others stepping in it. They just shake their tails and trot in the other direction like they weren't the ones who smelt it—*and* dealt it. *Plop!*

Horses, as it turns out, are kind of jerks.

And thanks to the queen's law, jerks were now everywhere—which meant their poop was everywhere. People refused to leave their homes because of the smell. Soon, it was decided that, like the poop outside, Queen Isabella's reign really, really *STUNK*.

CHAPTER 12
Jacob

"**F**or someone just crowned king, you sure seem like you're in a bad mood," Ms. Linda said to Jacob.

"I am," Jacob said. "All my favorite shows are finished for the season. That means I have nothing to watch for the next few months. What am I gonna do with my free time—READ A BOOK?!"

"Yes!" Ms. Linda said. "Reading is fun!"

It certainly is, as you, dear reader, can attest to—but probably only if you're reading a series of books about Classroom 13. But since Jacob was part of Classroom 13 (who was somehow an actual student now—which hardly makes sense), he couldn't read about himself. Now could he?

"You like TV, right?" 13 said.

"Boy, do I! It's my favorite thing in the whole world," Jacob answered.

13 said, "Well, now you're king. You can make a law that says your favorite TV shows *can't* go on break anymore and that they have to make more episodes right away. You can make it a law."

So King Jacob made a proclamation (which is a fancy word for an official, public statement): *"As of today, none of my favorite shows can go on break. They must keep going...forever!"*

Jacob called the TV people over in Hollywood on the phone and told them the news. "Your vacations are officially canceled. Get off the beach, nix your travel plans, and tell your families to unpack their bags. You're all going back to work to make more episodes of my favorite shows. I expect new episodes as soon as possible, so be prepared to work around the clock to make it happen, with *zero* bathroom breaks. Doesn't that sound fun?!"

It wasn't. Not for the TV people. Everyone had to pee really bad all of a sudden, and now they had to hold it. Plus, if they had to make shows forever, when did they get to go home?

Jacob's answer? "Never. This is their reward for making such great TV."

13

13 looked at the top of this page and noticed that it was the 13th chapter. Which meant it was 13's turn to be ~~king~~, *um*, I mean, ~~queen~~, *ur*, how about, ruler.

"Yup, that's me," 13 said. Its cube head glowed. 13 snapped its fingers, and a crown appeared.

"Hey, wait a minute! I thought Ms. Linda

said we were going in *alpha-flex-tubble* order," Liam said. (He had a hard time pronouncing "alphabetical.") "Since Jacob just went, that means it's Jayden's turn!"

"It's cool. You can go first, 13," Triple J said.

"What?!" Liam squealed. "If you're passing on your turn, then it should be *my* turn. I come next in roll call! It goes *J*, then *K*, then *L*. In fact, 13 is a number, not a letter, so I don't even know when he goes!"

"Liam brings up a good point," Ms. Linda said. "We agreed to go in *alphabetical* order, but I didn't account for 13, which is technically a number. I suppose we could go in *numerical* order, which would make 13's turn after Liam, who is the twelfth student to make a law...."

"Ms. Linda, you're being really confusing," Mason said. He showed her the beginning of this chapter. "See? It says 13. It's even listed in the table of contents! So it should be 13's chapter."

"I guess you're right," Ms. Linda said. "I can't

argue with the table of contents. Even if it really *isn't* a table."

13 was still adjusting to life as a human child. Sure, 13 had arms and legs like a *Homo sapiens* (that's the scientific name for "human") and wore clothes like its classmates, but 13 still thought of itself as a classroom.

"I'm not sure what kind of law I should make," 13 said to Lily and Ava.

"Well, what do *you* want?" Lily asked.

"Yeah, make a law that *you* would like!" Ava added.

13 thought about this for a minute. Then it remembered its favorite thing in the world....

13 took the royal podium and announced its new law. ***"From this day forth, every citizen of our fair country shall be <u>mopped</u> once a day!"***

People were confused. 13 added, "I know you will love the mopping law. It's going to be the

best thing you've ever experienced. You won't soon forget it!"

The crowd cheered. They didn't know what *"mopping"* was or what it meant, but they couldn't wait to have the *best thing they'd ever experience.*

Within the hour, people around the nation were chatting online, trying to guess what *"mopping"* meant. Some people thought it was a funny new word. Others thought it was an old word with a new meaning. But teachers pointed out that *"mopped"* was just an active past tense verb of *"mop,"* which means to clean something by wiping. Now everyone was just confused. "What does our ~~king~~ ~~queen~~ ruler 13 mean when it says we'll all be *mopped* once a day?"

Well, when a former-classroom-turned-human-child said *"mopped,"* 13 literally meant *mopped.*

You see, back when *13* was still *Classroom 13,* its favorite part of each day was the end of the day—when Mr. Bernard (the school janitor) would come and mop the floors. After a day of being stomped on by dirty shoes and filthy feet, getting *mopped* was like a warm shower for a classroom floor. It was like being made brand-new again. A fresh start. After getting *mopped*, Classroom 13 smelled like lemon-pine and sparkled like a diamond. This made 13 feel like the prettiest room in school.

13—who was now a human (sort of), who was also now the ~~king~~ ~~queen~~ ruler—wanted to share this wonderful, clean, refreshing, pretty feeling with the whole world. Who wouldn't want to have their whole body wiped with a mop and smell like lemon and pine? Who didn't want to get *mopped*?

By royal decree, an army of janitors entered people's homes and rubbed dirty mops all over people's faces and bodies. One by one, house by house, the janitorial army marched across the nation, with old mops and buckets of brown-gray mop water.

It turns out that human people are not like classrooms. They do *not* like being *mopped*. And what works to make a floor shine does not work to make a person shine.

Instead, it made people look like wet dogs. Hair would become matted and clothes would get sticky with floor gunk and old gum. Some would find loose coins in their ears; others would get wet dust bunnies in their noses. Skin was left feeling *slimy*.

Everyone, everywhere, started to look like... well, dirty floors.

If you listen closely, you can still hear people screaming things like: *"WHYYYYY????"* Or, *"EW!! MAKE IT STOP!!!"* Or, *"This is definitely NOT the best thing I've ever experienced!"*

These yelling fits could be heard all the way to the castle, where 13 thought people were screaming with joy. This made 13 smile.

Yes, 13 had a lot to learn about being human.

CHAPTER 14
Jayden Jason

Jayden Jason James—known to many of his friends at school as Triple J—was called Jason at home. His brothers' names were Jayden Justin, Jayden Jordan, and Jayden Jake. His sister's name was Jayden Pink. Can you tell his parents really liked the name Jayden?

At home, Jason mowed the grass once a week. He hated this chore. Grass always got all in his clothes and made him super itchy. But mowing

was the only way he could get his allowance—which was five dollars a week.

"Five dollars?!" he complained each time. "What can I buy with five dollars?"

"Not much," his sister said.

"When I was your age, my allowance was one *dollar* a week," his dad said.

"When I was your age, my allowance was one *quarter* a week," his grandfather said.

"When I was your age, my allowance was one *nothing* a week. That's right—I didn't even get an allowance!" his great-grandfather said. "So be grateful!"

Jason *was* grateful.

(But he still wanted more money.)

So when he became king, Jason decided to do something about it—and not just for himself, but for all kids who needed more money. Jason called a big meeting in front of the castle. Thousands gathered to hear the new king's decree.

"Hello, citizens! I've been thinking..." King Jason began. "Allowances are good, but they could be better. It's always nice to have a little extra spending cash. That way you can get a slice of pizza, or go to the movies, or buy those cool new shoes—you know, the ones that your parents won't buy you. But money is hard to come by. Especially when your dad makes you mow the grass for a meager *five* dollars a *week*.

"So, as of today, I am making a law: *Every person—under the age of fifteen—gets a daily allowance of ten dollars!*" King Jason declared. Everyone in the crowd—under the age of fifteen—cheered.

"Are you crazy?!" his advisors said, pulling him off the stage. "Ten dollars a day is seventy dollars a week, or three hundred dollars in an average month, or three thousand six hundred and fifty dollars a year—*per person!*"

"That doesn't sound like a lot," said Jason.

"There are over ten million children in this country. That means..." The advisors crunched numbers on their calculators to show him. The numbers kept getting bigger and bigger. The government was going to have to pay over $36,500,000,000 a year for his new law....

Jason passed out for a second. When he woke up, he gulped and said, "That's a lot of zeroes."

"Of course it is," his advisors said. "It's over *THIRTY-SIX BILLION* dollars."

Jason passed out again. When he woke up, he asked, "So what do I do?"

"Go out there and tell the people you take back that law."

Jason looked at the crowd. All the kids were so happy and cheery. He didn't want to ruin their day.

"I won't do it," he said. "I won't take it back. You'll just have to find some way to make it happen."

"Fine. We'll raise taxes," the advisors said. And they did.

When Jason went to buy a slice of pizza, it cost two dollars. And the tax on it was also two dollars. When Jason went to buy a movie ticket for ten dollars, the tax was also ten dollars. When he went to buy that new pair of shoes he wanted (that his parents wouldn't buy), they cost one hundred dollars. And the tax? Yup, another one hundred dollars.

"What gives?" Jason asked.

The advisors shrugged. "We made the taxes equal to everyone's spending."

Each and every person in the country was furious with Jason. Things were more expensive than ever. Food, gas, utilities, clothes, computers—everything was super-taxed!

He called another big meeting in front of the castle. This time, people threw slices of pizza and popcorn and old shoes at him.

When he got home, Benji and Fatima asked him to go to the movies. He looked in his pockets. He didn't have enough. He asked, "Dad, can I have my allowance money?"

"Sure..." his dad said, "*after* you mow the grass."

CHAPTER 15
Liam

When it came to pulling pranks, and farting, and causing all sorts of chaos in Classroom 13, Liam was a legend. He took pride in breaking rules and treated trouble like an art form. His schemes were his paintbrush, and the world was his canvas. (It was just one of the reasons he traded his pet llama for Chloe's pet crocodile. Crocodiles were far more troublemaking than llamas.)

After watching his fellow classmates *make* a bunch of laws, Liam decided to *break* a bunch of laws.

Liam took to the castle balcony and looked out over his citizens. "I am your king, and I'm here with a new rule: *There are no rules—not for me, I mean.* I'm gonna break every law in this kingdom, and there's nothing anyone can do to stop me!"

Cameras flashed. Reporters yelled out questions. But King Liam refused to answer anything. Instead, he unleashed his pet crocodile on all the newspeople. "Snack time, buddy!"

CHOMP! CHOMP!

(Don't worry. The reporters all escaped with their lives—though, sadly, *not* with all of their toes.)

"Time to break my first law: public decency!" King Liam stripped off his clothes and ran through the town totally naked. He had no shame, waving to people as he passed (and flashed) them. As citizens gasped and covered their eyes in shock, Liam just laughed and wiggled his bottom.

One reporter caught it on camera, and they showed it on the news. Liam's old British grandmum clutched her pearls. "Why, I've never seen such rude behavior! And to think we're related!"

"Time for my next law breaking!" Liam said, farting his way toward the public pool. He walked right past a sign that read:

NO RUNNING! NO DIVING! NO SPLASHING!
AND ABSOLUTELY NO PEEING IN THE POOL!

King Liam ran, then dove into the water, then splashed, and then...you guessed it.

Then King Liam went on a nonstop crime spree. He littered! He trespassed! He gambled! He downloaded music illegally! Liam fished without a permit! He even bribed a cop to buy him beer!! (Don't worry, it was just root beer,

which Liam could have bought himself, but you know, it's the principle of the matter.)

He rode his bike on the sidewalk! He let his pet crocodile poo on the sidewalk, and he did *not* clean it up! He drove a car (though only in the parking lot with his dad), but without a seat belt! He threw a loud dance party in the public library, right under the sign that read PLEASE BE QUIET! He even set off a bunch of illegal fireworks while jaywalking to an ice cream truck, where he took four Popsicles without paying! Liam laughed. "Three crimes in one! Triple threat!"

King Liam (still naked, by the way) was eating his stolen Raspberry Rocket Pops and trying to think of more laws he could break, when he noticed something strange. It was totally silent. The whole center of town didn't even have people....Wait, there they were!

People were locked in their cars or standing on top of mailboxes, or inside their stores, barricading their doors.

"Why are you hiding from me?" Liam asked. "I didn't mean to scare anybody. I just wanted to have some fun."

Ms. Linda, who had climbed all the way to the top of the lamppost, pointed behind Liam. He turned and read:

PLEASE KEEP ALL PETS ON LEASHES.
IT'S THE **LAW**.

Liam said, "But my pet crocodile is—"

"Right behind you!" Ms. Linda cried out.

It all became clear. People weren't hiding from Liam; they were hiding from his pet crocodile. The same crocodile that was pacing toward him with a wild look in its eye.

"Oh, hi, boy." King Liam chuckled nervously. "Looks like I broke the leash law, too, huh? Wasn't even trying for that one. Yay? You look hungry. Didn't those reporters' toes fill you up?"

The crocodile licked its fangs, then started after him.

Liam ran for his life, flashing his bottom to the whole town all over again. He shouted, "I'll never break the law again! I'll follow the rules! Especially the leash ones! I promise!! *AAAAHHHH!!!!*"

The next day, Liam's old British grandmum told reporters, "He got what was coming to him. My grandson acted a fool. He was a royal pain in the butt, so it was only fitting that his crocodile taught him what a real *pain in the butt* meant."

The reporters raised their hands to ask questions. One shouted, "Did King Liam lose one buttock or two?!"

Liam's grandmum smiled. "Let's just say he won't be getting *cheeky* anytime soon."

CHAPTER 16
Lily

Lily hated barfing more than anything. When she became queen, she tried to outlaw barfing. But her advisors insisted the government had no control over "bodily functions."

Lily had to consider a new law to make. She'd always wanted to go into space. So instead, she announced, *"I am opening the nation's first free space camp school—where any kid can learn to be an astronaut."*

"It sounds expensive," said the advisors.

"I don't care. Spare no expense," Lily commanded. The advisors tried to talk her out of it. But Lily did not back down. Within a week, space camp school opened in Cape Canaveral, Florida. Lily was its first student.

"I want to learn everything," she told the instructors. "Don't go easy on me."

And they didn't.

Every day was an eighteen-hour-long school day. Lily learned about zero-gravity conditions in space, how to grow potatoes on Mars, and how to send e-mails from one planet to another. They taught her how to engineer robotics, navigate through an asteroid belt, and fly a rocket. They also made her learn really hard math. (Lily didn't even like math.)

Lily learned the first living creatures to go into space were *not* people—they were *fruit flies*. In 1947, fruit flies were sent into space along with some seeds of corn. (True story). In 1957,

Laika—a stray dog from the streets of Moscow, Russia—was the first dog in space. (Also a true story.) In 1959, two monkeys—named Able and Miss Baker—went into space. (Totally true story. Don't believe me? Look it up!)

Lily had no idea that fruit flies, dogs, and monkeys had been to space before humans. She was astonished. But if they could do it, how hard could it be?

"Can I go to space now?" Lily asked.

"I'm afraid not, Queen Lily," said one of the instructors. "You haven't passed all the tests required of astronauts yet."

"What else do I have to do?"

"Well, for one thing, you still need high-g training...."

A big smile spread across Lily's face. "High-g training is the one with the centrifuge, right?"

"That's the one." Her instructors explained, "You see, when astronauts fly into space, their bodies must be able to withstand great forces.

Sometimes the forces are so great, they will lose consciousness. So by putting them in a centrifuge, and spinning them around faster and faster and faster, we help them get used to it."

"I love spinning rides at amusement parks," said Lily. "Strap me in!"

"We recommend not eating before the ride," her instructor said. "Did you eat lunch?"

Lily had waited long enough to get here. She wasn't going to let a silly little rule get in the way. So she lied. "Nope."

Then the scientists strapped Lily into the centrifuge—the giant machine that was going to spin her around so fast and so hard, it would feel like she was being shot into space. The instructors buckled her up nice and tight.

"Are you ready for this, Queen Lily?"

"I've never been more ready," she said.

The centrifuge began to spin. It went faster and faster. At first, Lily was laughing. Then she felt her face pushing back. Her whole body was flattened against the back of her seat. She felt like a pancake.

After a few minutes, the centrifuge stopped. Lily unbuckled herself and hopped out. She was standing still, but it felt like the whole room was spinning. That's when she barfed.

Thankfully, Lily got her helmet off in time, or she would have puked inside her space suit. Instead, she vomited across the room. After that, she kept barfing, right into her helmet.

"I'm so embarrassed," she said, trying not to cry. She wanted to be tough for the astronaut instructors.

"Don't worry about it!" they said. "Astronauts puke in space all the time. It's part of space sickness."

"Space sickness?" Lily said.

"Yeah, it's like motion sickness on a boat— only way worse."

"Astronauts throw up? All the time?" Lily asked in a whisper.

"Yup. And if you think that's bad, let me tell you how they go to the bathroom—"

"Please don't!" Lily wiped some barf from her chin as her tummy rumbled. "Um, maybe not right now. I think maybe I need a break."

Lily was right. She did need a break, which was fine. Space wasn't going anywhere....

CHAPTER 17
Mark

Mark isn't just the most handsome kid in class, he's also pretty smart. When he became king, he thought of a fantastic new law:

"Two days for a weekend are not enough," he declared. "So *I'm reversing the week. Weekdays are now only Monday and Tuesday—the rest of the days are now the weekend!!*"

The nation went wild. Everyone cheered. He was quickly nominated as "Best! King! Ever!"

King Mark went further. He announced weekly parties called TGIT—"Thank Goodness It's Tuesday!" He also insisted all schools be closed for the "New Weekend," meaning Wednesday, Thursday, Fartday, Saturday, and Sunday.

(What's that? What do you mean I misspelled Friday? No, I didn't. You're crazy. No, I'm not. You are!)

The people were ecstatic (that's a fancy word for "super happy")...

...but only at first. See, no one was working anymore. Everyone was off for five days of the week. That meant the mail didn't arrive on time, pizza parlors were closed all the time, and garbage started to pile up on the streets.

With everyone only working two days a week, things started to fall apart. Businesses didn't make money. So they stopped paying people. That meant parents didn't have money for the kids, and that meant no money for zoos, pools, skating rinks, amusement parks, movie theaters, or anything fun....

People had five days off, but nothing to do. The nation started to crumble. And everyone blamed Mark. They decided to revoke his law and take away his crown.

"No, not my crown! It looks so perfect and beautiful on my head!" he cried. He had to think of a new law, and fast. King Mark declared, "Monday is the worst. It's the day after a weekend, and the first day of the rest of the week. But no more! *I am declaring every Monday a national holiday! They can be called Mark Mondays!*"

But it was too late. They'd taken his crown, and he had no power to make laws anymore.

It's too bad. I think Mark had a really great idea. A four-day week and a three-day weekend sounds pretty nice to me. What do *you* think?

CHAPTER 18
Mason

One thing about Mason is that he loves tacos. As soon as he heard former king Mark declare Mark Mondays, it gave him an idea. *"I declare that our school cafeteria serve tacos on Tuesdays. We'll call it Taco Tuesdays!"*

"But, Mason," Ms. Linda said, "they already do that."

"Perfect!" Mason said. "My job as king is done."

CHAPTER 19
Mya & Madison

"**A**re you thinking what I'm thinking?" Mya asked her twin sister, Madison.

"Yes! I always am, silly. Because we're twins!" Madison replied.

"On the count of three, say it...ONE..."

"...*TWO*..."

"*THREE—*"

Both girls at the exact same time, *"CASTLE MAKEOVER!!!"*

After giggling about that for almost an hour, the twin queens ordered the staff to repaint the castle from ceiling to floor. And what color do you think the twins chose for that? You guessed it. *Princess Pink.*

Using ten tons of glitter and twenty tons of shiny plastic rhinestones, the twins bedazzled the entire castle. This meant using leaf blowers to blow glitter and rhinestones *everywhere* and on *everything*. The castle now looked like a giant hot-pink disco ball.

"What about making a new law?" Ms. Linda asked.

Madison & Mya shrugged. "What's the point? All people care about is what's pretty."

CHAPTER 20
Olivia

Olivia loved school more than any other kid on the planet. If she could go to school seven days a week, she would.

So it should come as no surprise that she made this a reality when she became queen. "I'm changing the school laws. We don't need school five days a week—"

"Yay!" Teo cheered.

"Best queen ever!" Isabella squealed.

"Less school, more fun!" Fatima added.

"Preach, sister!" Mason shouted with glee.

Olivia continued: "—we need school *seven days a week!* My new law: ***School will now be every single day***," she announced to her classmates with a big smile.

They were NOT smiling back.

"But when will we have time to go shopping?" Preeya asked.

"Or make number two?" Liam said, followed by a fart.

"Or hang with our friends?!" Ava added.

"Ou regarder des films français?" Hugo asked.

Queen Olivia was getting the sense that her classmates (and the country) were unhappy about her new law. "Look, from seven in the morning until midnight, we'll have class. That gives you seven whole hours to do homework and eat, sleep, shower, floss, see your friends and family, and organize your homework for the next day. Best news ever, right?!"

Everyone protested. Every kid in the country voted to try Olivia for treason. The result was unanimous: Olivia was no longer queen.

She may have been a genius, but she had a lot to learn about being a kid.

CHAPTER 21
Preeya

Preeya was used to getting what she wanted—which is why she said her recent birthday party was *"awful and stuuuuuupid."* Her words, not mine.

(Oh, you didn't know about Preeya's party? Neither did I. I guess our invitations were "lost" in the mail.)

At this party that you and I ~~missed~~ weren't invited to, Preeya got lots of gifts: concert tickets, new outfits, jewelry, some books about Classroom 13, a karaoke machine, money, and a brand-new bike. Still, she told her friends that her party was *"awful and stuuuuuupid."* Why? Apparently, her parents didn't get her the gift she really wanted.

"My birthday is like, *so...totally...ruined!!!*" Preeya cried.

"But you had a wonderful party and so many people came, and everyone brought gifts," her dad countered.

"But I didn't get what I really wanted...." Preeya whined. "I wanted *a car!*"

"You're too young to drive!" her mom said.

"It'd be illegal!" her dad said.

Preeya shouted, "I hate the law. I want to drive!"

I bet you can guess what she did when she became queen. (What? No, she did not demand pancakes! I think *you* are the one demanding pancakes. Now, where was I? Oh, yes...)

Preeya announced: "As your new queen, *I am changing the legal driving age from sixteen years old to eight years old.*"

Within twenty-four hours, half the nation's cars were filled with drivers who couldn't see over the steering wheel. And Preeya was one of them. As she hopped into her car and drove away, her parents shouted, "Come back! You don't know *how* to drive!"

How hard can it be? Preeya thought. *I bet it's just like riding a bike.*

First, she plowed through a neighbor's yard and killed a bunch of garden gnomes. (Technically, they weren't really alive because they were made of plastic, but still.)

Then Preeya stopped paying attention to the road when she got a text message. She crashed into a tree. (Don't worry—she could barely reach the gas pedal, so she wasn't going very fast.)

Next, Preeya decided to visit her friend Olivia. She drove the car straight through the side of Olivia's house. She crashed right into Olivia's bedroom. (Luckily, Olivia had been in the kitchen.)

"Olivia, are you home?" Preeya asked.

"You destroyed my room!" Olivia shouted.

Preeya said, "It's just a little scratch!"

(It wasn't.)

"Maybe I should go."

(She did.)

Finally, Preeya decided to drive to the mall. But her phone rang. She took the call from her friend Ava. While she was on the phone, she noticed in the rearview mirror that her hair was a mess. She let go of the steering wheel to fix it.

(Dear reader, when you're old enough to drive, make sure you never let go of the steering wheel.)

Preeya crashed right into a delivery truck. Don't worry. Everyone was okay. The delivery truck driver hopped out and asked, "Are you okay?"

"I'm fine, but my car is wrecked!"

"Hey, you're Queen Preeya, ain't ya?" the deliveryman asked.

Preeya nodded. He handed her a slip of paper. It was an official-looking document from the castle.

"Is this an award for beautiful driving?" Preeya asked.

"No," the truck driver said. "It's a notice of termination. Your new driving law is a disaster. The country fired you."

"But I don't want to be fired," Preeya whined.

The truck driver laughed. "Welcome to life. You can't always get what you want."

CHAPTER 22
Santiago

While they would never say this to his face, some people thought Santiago wasn't fit to be king. He was often sick, and currently he was still inside a big plastic bubble.

"My doctors tell me it's only temporary!" Santiago said. "Don't you worry about me, I'll—*cough*—be the—*achooooooooo!!*—healthiest king you've—*sniffle*—ever seen."

"Are you sure you don't want me to call the school nurse?" Ms. Linda asked.

"Why not call the best doctors in the land and tell them to report to the palace at once?" Santiago said. "Because as king, I am making a new law—*sniffle—I'm giving everyone, every-where—cough—FREE HEALTH CARE—achooo!!*"

The whole country agreed: Seeing a doctor *should* be free. Being healthy shouldn't be a luxury—it should be a right. Expensive medical bills would become a thing of the past. Per Santiago's new law, doctors had to treat any sick person free of charge. And medicine was free, too.

Santiago was still inside his plastic bubble, but he refused to miss a press conference. He told the crowd of reporters: "No one should have to pay for being sick. Just ask my mom—she could fill the Atlantic Ocean with my doctor bills. Even with insurance, it's still pricey. It shouldn't be."

While Santiago felt *down* about still being sick, his popularity kept going straight *up*. People loved him as their king. He was praised in the media for his free-health-care law and viewed as a hero by those who normally couldn't afford to see a doctor when they needed one most.

People who were sick? Cured. Broken bones? In casts. Need a doctor's visit? Don't worry about the bill. The sick were now healthy and could afford to enjoy life like everyone else. And it was all thanks to the King Inside the Bubble.

Everyone wanted to honor King Santiago and personally thank him for helping those in need. Offers poured in from famous talk show hosts. World leaders wanted to host him in their home countries. Rock stars wanted to put on a concert for him. Even his fellow classmates staged a play to celebrate his reign. It was based on his life story, titled: *Saint-iago: The Story of the Generous Bubble King.*

The Classroom 13 students reserved Santiago a front-row seat for their first performance—but he couldn't make it. In fact, he wasn't able to go to any of those fancy-sounding fun events mentioned above.

Why?

Because even with free doctor visits and free medicine, there was just no cure for being Santiago, who seemed to catch everything.

He was still had the nasty stomach-throat-skin-virus thing, and he wasn't allowed to leave the castle to do anything fun. It was strict bed rest for the next month. Doctor's orders.

CHAPTER 23
Sophia

Did you know that seven billion trees get cut down each year? It's true. Look it up. (And don't feel bad. I didn't know, either.)

Well, Sophia knew that, along with about a zillion other ~~trivia~~ *tree*-via facts about the rain forest. If you met her, she'd tell you herself—even if you didn't ask her. She loved to talk about the environment, especially about saving it from

humanity. (Who do you think cuts down the trees?)

Now that Sophia was queen, she had a plan.

"I am your queen, and by royal decree, *I demand that every person on this planet plant one tree today, and one tree each year thereafter.* If every human on the planet plants just one tree a year, we might actually start saving the planet rather than destroying it. There are over seven billion people on this planet. If we work together, we can make the world a better place."

"That's actually...a really good law," Ms. Linda said. She was impressed.

Sophia rounded up all her fellow students and handed each one a small tree sapling. "Are you ready to work?" she asked.

"I don't like working," said Preeya.

"I don't want to get dirt under my nails," said Mark.

"What if we'd rather spend our afternoon

juggling harmonicas while riding a unicycle?" Mason asked.

"Anyone who doesn't want to plant trees can stay here and listen to me recite every piece of conservation *tree*-via I know," Queen Sophia said. "Like, did you know there are over two hundred and fifty thousand known plant species that—"

Whoosh!

The entire class ran outside and started working before Sophia could go on and on about the environment again. (Sophia knew people hated hearing all the factoids—so much, in fact, it proved quite motivational.)

So the students of Classroom 13 spent the day planting young trees. At the end of the day, everyone was pretty proud of their work.

Have you planted a tree this year? You should. And get your friends and family to do one, too. Heck, maybe ask your teacher to plant a tree.

(I'm totally serious. You can even show her this book and tell her Honest Lee said it was a good idea.)

Saving the planet starts with you. Yes, YOU, the kid holding this book. You better be-*leaf* it.

CHAPTER 24
Teo

Teo was not allowed to watch R-rated movies. He wasn't even allowed to watch PG-13 ones. His parents had very strict rules about what he could and couldn't watch on TV and at the movies.

"I don't see what the big deal is!" he argued with his mom and dad. "So there's a little bit of violence. Or maybe a few bad words. Or maybe

some naked people. Who cares?! Eventually, I'll see and hear all that stuff anyway, right?"

His mom and dad shook their heads. "The answer is NO!"

So when Teo became king, he knew exactly what law to make. He walked to the royal podium and tapped on the microphone. "Is this thing on?"

All the reporters nodded. "I am changing the law. *No more age restrictions on movies! Kids can see whatever movie they want—and parents can't stop them!*"

"King Teo, sir," said one of the reporters, "I don't think that's an actual law."

"Try to tell my parents that," Teo said.

"No, really, it's *not* a law," said another reporter.

"Exactly," Teo noted. "Not anymore."

When Teo got home, his parents both said, "You're still not allowed to watch R-rated movies."

"I'm the king!" he shouted. Then he rode his bike to the movie theater with all his allowance money. He watched every single R-rated movie they had showing.

He saw an adult spy movie with lots of blood and guts. (It made Teo barf in his popcorn.) He saw an adult romantic comedy. (He didn't get any of the jokes.) And he saw a foreign film. (He didn't understand a single word.)

Then he watched all the horror movies. One was about an alien that ate people. The next was about a monster that ate people. And then he watched one about a crazy clown...who ate people.

As Teo left the theater, he realized he had to ride his bike home alone. Everything seemed darker than usual, and all the shadows looked like aliens and monsters and crazy clowns. So he called his parents and asked if they would come pick him up.

"Are you okay?" his mom asked.

Teo wasn't sure. That night, he couldn't sleep. His head was filled with too many scary thoughts. Every time he heard the wind blow, or the house creak, or a mouse walk across the floorboards, he sat up and tried not to scream.

The next morning at breakfast, his sister asked, "How'd you sleep?"

"*Sleep?!*" Teo asked, shaking and looking around the room for aliens or monsters or crazy clowns. "After what I saw, I'll never sleep again."

CHAPTER 25
~~Touchdown~~ The Teacher's Assistant

"Hello," 13 said to ~~Touchdown~~ Mandy, the new teacher's assistant. "I know you're not technically a student, but would you like a turn at being queen?"

~~Touchdown~~ Mandy said, "*Moo.*"

"How rude!" 13 said, deeply offended.

Then ~~Touchdown~~ Mandy ate some grass.

No new laws were made that day. The nation was thankful.

CHAPTER 26
William

William didn't trust people. Or the government. Or anybody. He had conspiracy theories about pretty much everything. And any little thing could set him off: sunscreen, stray dogs, helicopters, even dust. Today, the thing that bothered him most? Washing his hands.

"I read online that too much hand washing can make you sick," William explained to 13.

"Something about soap killing all the good germs that help the body fight off all the bad germs."

"I've only been a sorta-human for a very little while," 13 said, "but I'm pretty sure you shouldn't believe everything you read on the Internet."

"What do you know?!" William shouted.

Some would say William was ~~paranoid~~ suspicious, but I believe some healthy distrust is good. The key word being "some." After all, the Internet is filled with "fake news." So make sure to consider where you get your information from. Definitely don't get your facts from the same website William did:

"The Best Fake News on the Internet!"

But William will be William. Which is why he stopped washing his hands entirely. When he became king, he declared: ***"I ban all mandatory hand washing."***

People weren't sure how to feel about that.

The next day, William's grandparents took him to their favorite Mexican restaurant. "I'm going to the bathroom," William said.

"Don't forget to wash your hands," his grandmother said.

"Never!" he shouted.

I wish I could tell you William washed his hands after touching the *icky, stinky toilet handle*. But he did not.

William went back to the table and started eating salty chips and salsa. He licked his fingers a lot. Then he ate enchiladas—made by restaurant cooks who didn't wash their hands at all that day.

That night, it wasn't William's ~~paranoia~~ distrust that kept him up through the night—it was his stomach. He was up and out of bed every five minutes to use the bathroom. (Stuff was coming out *both* ends, if you know what I mean.) Poor William thought he was dying. He certainly felt like it. It was the worst case of parasites and food poisoning the royal doctors had ever seen.

The doctors shook their heads and said, "You gonna undo that law now?"

William nodded yes. He also made a promise to himself to *always* wash his hands.

CHAPTER 27
Ximena

Ximena adjusted the crown on her head, then announced, *"I want a royal wedding!"* It wasn't exactly a "law," but Ximena was queen and that's what she wanted. So she got it.

Everyone everywhere agreed that royal weddings were wonderfully fun. All citizens were given the day off so they could throw their own royal-wedding-watching parties or come see the festivities in person.

As the morning arrived, every channel in the kingdom was broadcasting the ceremony. It was the biggest televised event since...well, *ever*.

Reporters tried to guess who the lucky husband-to-be was. There were lots of hunches. When asked, all the kings and queens of Classroom 13 had different opinions. Ava thought it would be "a YouTube celebrity famous for, you know, stuff." Preeya wanted it to be "an attractive prince, of course!" Sophia hoped he would be "a rich aristocrat with an air of mystery." Liam guessed, "A toad—but like an actual toad, not a prince in disguise." (Oh, Liam.) Isabella suggested, "A dark and handsome cowboy." Mark said, "A dark and handsome cowboy," and then he blushed.

When the music began, Ximena walked out in the most beautiful white dress you've ever seen. Her family was moved to tears. "Such a beautiful bride," they all cried. She walked down the aisle as white rose petals fluttered down from above. It was like something out of a fairy tale. There was only one problem.

"Uh...where's the groom?" the officiant asked the bride.

Ximena scrunched up her face and said, "*Ew! I'm too young to get actually married. I just wanted a royal wedding and a royal dress and a royal wedding cake. Is that so wrong?*"

The nation felt *bamboozled*. (That's a fancy word that means fooled or tricked.) That is, until they tasted the cake. Ximena made sure everyone in the country got a slice. It was the best cake anyone had ever had.

CHAPTER 28
Yuna

Yuna did *not* want to be the queen.

She wanted to be the queen's *spy*.

So when it was her turn to become queen, Yuna gave herself a super top secret spy mission. (She—of course—gave it to herself in code.) After the mission was made official, Yuna demoted herself from world leader to secret agent.

Her mission was this:

UOB GL GSV MLIGS KLOV
RM Z HFKVIHLMRX QVG,
KZIZXSFGV WLDM GL Z
HMLD NLGLIXBXOV, GSVM
URMW Z KLOZI YVZI
MZNVW GVW. SV DROO
VHXLIG BLF GL GSV OZHG
HVXIVG SRWVLFG LU GSV
ZORVM ORAZIW MZARH
UILN KOZMVG C. KFG
LOREV QFRXV RM GSVRI
DZGVI GZMP. ZORVM
ORAZIW MZARH ZIV
ZOOVITRX GL LOREVH.
RG'OO NZPV GSVN HRXP,
ZMW GSVB'OO ZOO SZEV
GL OVZEV LFI KOZMVG.

106

CHAPTER 29
Zoey

Zoey's last name was Zucchini, but she wasn't green. She was actually bright red—thanks to a terrible sunburn. Zoey was one of those unlucky people with fair skin that burns instantly if she doesn't slather herself in sunscreen and hide in the shade.

Unfortunately her dad chose a beach vacation, and Zoey fell asleep in the sun. Four hours, and Zoey was as burnt as toast. Zoey hated the sun.

"You burned me on purpose!" she screamed at the sun. It didn't say anything. Because, you know, it's the sun. And it doesn't speak. Still, Zoey took the sun's silence as being rude, and she vowed revenge.

So, when she became queen, she did what any rational sun-hating queen would do: She soothed her sunburn with aloe vera and said, *"I royally command that <u>the sun</u> be made illegal!"*

You read that right. Zoey wanted the sun gone, and she didn't care how. But her royal advisors and the royal scientists and even the royal army said they couldn't help her. So she went to 13. "You have magical powers or something, right? Can you make the sun disappear from the sky forever?"

"I could, but that'd be really bad because of gravity and the planets and stuff."

"Well, could you make sunlight go away?"

"I can do that, too, but people need the sun. So do plants. The whole world kind of needs it to make everything work. Plus, people are finally using solar energy, and that's good for the planet."

Zoey pitched a tantrum. "Just do it, 13! Use those magic lips to make an eclipse. Or else!" Zoey raised her fist like she was going to hit 13.

13 had never been hit before. The threat of violence was pretty scary. So without thinking further, 13 just did it.

Right then and there, at just a few minutes after noon, the moon moved in front of the sun, and the nation was suddenly covered in complete darkness.

At first, people thought it was cool. Schoolchildren everywhere rushed to make those eclipse-watching thingies out of cereal boxes and foil and tape. (Why? Because you're *not* supposed to look directly at an eclipse, silly.

It's really bad for your eyes. I'm serious! Look it up.)

Farmers worried about their crops. They asked, "How will I grow my corn?"

Sailors lost their way in the water. They cried, "How will we find our way home?" (With a compass, you silly gooses.)

But all the vampires cheered for the twenty-four-hour darkness! They said, "How will we decide who to bite first? Woo-hoo! Let's party!"

Vampires overran the whole country.

And the citizens of the queens and kings of Classroom 13? Well, they'd had enough. It was time for a revolution.

What's a rev-o-lu-tion? It's an instance of revolt. Or in this case, a forcible overthrow of the government. They were going to get rid of the queens and kings of Classroom 13....

CHAPTER 30
The Former Kings and Queens of Classroom 13

All the kings and queens were sitting around in their throne room, taking a break from weeks of making laws. (It was exhausting work.) Suddenly, they heard loud noises coming from outside the castle. Mark looked out the window. "Uh-oh. That doesn't look good."

"What?" Preeya asked.

"There's an angry mob outside chanting,

'Down with crazy kings and kooky queens! Down with ridiculous royalty! Off with their heads!'"

The kids all ran to the windows to see for themselves. Tens of thousands of people were gathered outside the castle with pitchforks and torches.

"What are those pitchforks for?" Emma asked.

"Maybe they're here to garden," Mason said.

"We're *not* here to garden!" one protester shouted back. "We're here to take away your crowns and fix the nation!"

Another protester added: "Yeah! There's horse poop everywhere—"

Another protestor added, "Underage drivers crashing into everything!"

Even Liam's grandmum was in the crowd. She threw a tomato at her grandson. "I saw Liam's exposed bottom—despicable!"

"You got rid of sunlight! No one can see anything or get a sweet summer tan! And there are vampires everywhere!" another protestor shouted.

"You are all, by far, the *worst rulers* in the history of humanity!"

Mason recognized this woman. "Mom? Stop it! You're embarrassing me in front of my friends!"

His mom waved. "After I dethrone you, let's go get some ice cream, okay?" Then she went back to shouting mean stuff and angrily waving her torch.

The kids all looked at one another with worry. *Gulp!*

"Well, students, I suppose this little educational experiment is over. We should probably get back to school," Ms. Linda said. "What do you think, Mandy?"

"*Moooo!*" ~~Touchdown~~ the teacher's assistant said.

"I couldn't have said it better myself," Ms. Linda noted. She'd never had such a wonderful teacher's aide before. "I'm thinking of hiring you full-time," she told the cow.

"*Moooooo*," ~~Touchdown~~ the teacher's assistant said.

"You heard Mandy—back on the bus! The field trip is over!" Ms. Linda started collecting crowns. "And, 13, please put everything back the way it was."

"Can I keep the mopping law?"

"No, 13."

"Okay, Ms. Linda." 13 snapped its fingers and magically undid all the chaos. The sun was no longer eclipsed. All the horse poop vanished, replaced by smog from cars. Liam got his butt cheeks back, and Liam's crocodile went back to the wild. 13 fixed all the chaos that the Classroom 13 students had created. The damage was undone.

The vampires were super bummed out. "The sun is out again? Boo! Hiss!"

And citizens were happy once again. Well, not happy exactly. I mean, the government isn't exactly perfect—but what is?

★ ★ ★

During the long bus ride back, the students were all chatting about what they'd done. Some, like Sophia, were proud of their royal accomplishments. "We planted a ton of new trees!"

"And we gave people free health care!" Santiago said from his quarantine bubble.

Others felt bad for the way they'd ruled. Teo said, "I'm gonna have R-rated nightmares for the rest of my life."

Preeya admitted, "I could have made the world a better place—if only I'd made my reign as queen last forever."

Ms. Linda sat back, almost proud. None of the students were on the phone. Instead, they were all talking about government and law making. Maybe they would really learn something. She got so excited that she broke up the conversation by asking, "What did everyone learn today?"

A hush fell over the bus.

Crickets.

(Which is a funny way of saying total silence.)

Finally, Mason raised a hand.

Ms. Linda called on him: "Yes, Mason—"

"I learned that tomorrow is Taco Tuesday."

"Tomorrow's Wednesday, bro," Mark corrected him. "Wednesday comes *after* Tuesday."

"Oh. Okay," Mason said. "There you go. I just learned Wednesday comes after Tuesday."

Ms. Linda sighed. "Well, at least that's something."

CHAPTER 31
Your Chapter

Grab some paper and a writing utensil. (Not a banana, silly. Try a pencil or pen.) Or if you have one of those fancy computer doohickeys, use that. Now, tell me...

If *YOU* were king or queen, what laws would you make—or break?

When you're done writing your chapter, share it with your teacher and your family, and, of course, your friends. (Don't forget your pets. Pets like to hear stories, too, you know.)

And if you're feeling particularly adventurous, send your story to the author. He'll get a kick out of them. (No, really, I'll give him a kick. Honestly. Wait...*I'm* the author, so *I* would have to kick *myself*. Never mind. No kicks. But send me your stories.)

HONEST LEE

LITTLE, BROWN BOOKS FOR YOUNG READERS
1290 AVENUE OF THE AMERICAS
NEW YORK, NY 10104

THE
and Heinous
HAPPY HALLOWEEN OF
CLASSROOM 13

Honest Lee and Matthew J. Gilbert

Meet PETER POWERS!

A boy whose superpowers are a little different from the rest.

 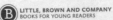